DEAD END

A collection of short stories

DEAD END

love. life. relationships.

Padmesh Gupta

यात्रा

YATRA BOOKS

An imprint of Vani Prakashan Group

vaniprakashan.com

First Edition 2024

YATRA BOOKS
VANI PRAKASHAN GROUP

Head Office

4695, 21-A, Daryaganj, New Delhi-110 002, India
Phone : +91 11 23273167, 11 23275710

Registered Bookstores and Offices

Ashok Rajpath, Patna-800 004, Bihar
Coffee House Campus, Mahatma Gandhi Marg, Allahabad-211 001, Uttar Pradesh
Mahatma Gandhi International Hindi University, Wardha-442 001, Maharashtra
36-A, Shakespeare Sarani, Near Rani Birla Girls College, Kolkata-700017, West Bengal

sales@vaniprakashan.in
vaniprakashan@gmail.com

Dead End
by Padmesh Gupta

ISBN : 978-93-5518-901-1
Collection of short-stories

Price : ₹ 295
£ 5
$ 9

Printed and bound in India at City Press, Delhi-110 095

Vani Prakashan's signature motif is created by Artist Maqbool Fida Husain

To

Oxford Business College

For all those who have enriched my life & encouraged my literary journey over two dynamic decades with the College

Contents

Unacceptance

"My heart, my soul will always belong to you, Sameer. You will always be with me like a shadow... always...," Anisha whispered, her voice trembling with emotion.

Tears cascaded down Sameer's cheeks, his heart shattered into a million pieces. "How will I live without you, Anisha? Every dawn begins with your name, every moment of mine passes with your name echoing in my soul."

"Please, Sameer, try to be sensible... Can you marry prior to your elder brother's wedding, and before settling into a new job? And how can I hold my younger sister Sunaina's marriage for my own desires? You are also aware of the white patches she has on her face, which doesn't help. As long as I remain single, my father won't consider her marriage. How can I break off her engagement and ruin her life? The weight of guilt would crush me."

"Anisha, without me... will you be able to live and wipe out our memories along with precious moments that we have shared?"

"No... never, Sameer. But my soul will always be intertwined with yours. In every racing beat of my heart eternally aching for you. You will never be far from my thoughts. Honestly, I don't feel as if I'm leaving you. We'll always stay connected. My love for you will remain unchanged, despite the distance. Promise me, Sameer, promise me you'll never make me feel like a stranger," Anisha pleaded, her voice breaking as she began to sob.

In that moment, Sameer and Anisha were enveloped in an emotional whirlwind, their hearts entwined in a bond stronger than any force on earth.

Incessant ringing of the doorbell brings Anisha back to reality – her dream shattered. A dream which often took Anisha back to her past.

Rajiv is standing at the door. "You still aren't ready! It's Avinash and Kalpana's anniversary. It will take at least two hours to reach Boston."

"I'm so sorry, Raj, I was feeling dizzy, just give me ten more minutes, I'll be ready soon," Anisha responded.

"Uff... these women, they relax at home all day and wait for their husbands to come home after a hard day's work." Rajiv grumbled, sitting on the couch.

The box of *sindoor* (vermilion) lying on the dressing table often reminded Anisha of her aunt Vandana's words on her wedding day,"Ani, today, your past has burnt in the flames of the holy fire. Rajiv is your new beginning. We are all strangers now, and Rajiv is everything to you until death do you part. His happiness is your happiness, his sorrow is your sorrow. This mark of *sindoor* is the symbol of your existence together.

Anisha put a small dot of *sindoor* on her forehead and looked at her reflection in the mirror, and for a moment felt as if Sameer flown past and kissed her forehead.

Anisha closed her eyes and then came out at the third call from Rajiv. "How do I look?"

"Come on, Anisha, Let's go." Rajiv, ignoring Anisha's question, walked out.

Anisha remembered Sameer's habit. Whenever Anisha met him, he used to gaze at her for a few moments, then often admire Anisha's clothes and praise her beauty.

Soon Rajiv and Anisha's car sped on the American highway between Long Island and Boston. Neon lit tall buildings nor the fashionable areas were able to quieten her turmoiled heart.

"It's been more than a year since the wedding. When are we going to India?" Anisha asked almost every day, receiving same toneless reply each time from Rajiv, "After you get your green card." Anisha's face would wilt and fade each day. Anisha's spirit was suffocating in this artificial life. She couldn't remove Sameer from her mind. American parties, artificial hustle-bustle, engaging in business talks, didn't appeal to Anisha.

Rajiv is a successful doctor in Long Island. Despite all the comforts and luxuries, Anisha is unable to distance herself from Sameer's memory and loneliness tugs at her heart.

Lost in her thoughts, Anisha didn't even realise when they reached Boston to attend the grand party at Holiday Inn for their friends anniversary. Anisha had to endure another evening immersed in music, dance, and a fashionable soiree.

Suddenly, a voice from behind startled Anisha. "Hey... Anisha... you here!"

"Sarika... What a pleasant surprise, when did you come to America?"

"A week ago, got into Boston University, doing my PhD. How are you?"

Today, after a long time, Anisha's face lit up as if a flower had blossomed. Both friends got lost in old memories. As soon as Sameer's mention came up, Sarika fell silent for a moment. Then, breaking the silence, she said,

"Anisha, lovers like Sameer are rare. Hey... do you want his email address?"

"Has he got email now? How delightful!" Anisha felt as if she had found a new life. In the meantime, Rajiv, approaching from behind, introduced himself to Sarika by touching Anisha's shoulders, "Hello, I'm Rajiv, Anisha's husband."

Anisha immediately introduced Sarika to Rajiv with a cheerful tone. "How do you like my friend?" Sarika asked Rajiv.

"First-class, Anisha is such a calm and quite girl, only the lucky ones find such a gem. She just talks a little less," Rajiv said, smiling as he looked at Anisha.

Sarika was perplexed for a moment. "Anisha was famous in college for her talkative nature, why this sudden change?"

While returning from the party, Anisha's hand reached out to hold Rajiv's. Rajiv felt invigorated by her touch. Anisha sat comfortably in her seat, resting her head on the headrest, lost in thoughts of Sameer with her eyes closed. After so many days, today, there was some hope was triggered about Sameer. Today, for the first time, Rajiv saw a glow on Anisha's face.

Suddenly, Anisha opened her eyes and said surprised, "Rajiv; how comes you are driving in the slow lane today? This is surely a surprise.

How many times have I requested you to control your speed!

"Yes, Anisha, I don't feel like going home. Today, seeing the glow on your face, feeling the touch of your hands; I just want to keep at a snail pace," Rajiv replied softly.

Anisha smiled and unfastened her seatbelt, reached over and nestled her head into his shoulder, pressing her inviting lips into his aftershave drenched neck. With an excited left hand on the steering wheel, he fondled her hair playfully.

Throughout the night, Rajiv savoured the fragrance of Anisha's alluring body, while Anisha, with closed eyes, came alive in the fragrance of Sameer's memories. She is now married to Rajiv, so her body was his as respect to tradition but in essence she only belongs to Sameer.

This was not the first night when Anisha's body was honouring the relationship of husband and wife, but her mind was aligning with Sameer's memories. Even on the wedding night with Rajiv, it was Sameer she dreamt of in a red *kurta*. Rajiv's body quenched its thirst and moved ahead but all Anisha was waiting for was the moment when she could go to Mumbai and meet Sameer.

In the morning, as soon as Rajiv left, Anisha sat down to write a love letter to Sameer via email. Sameer was overjoyed to reconnect. Modern age technology had brought the separated lovers together once again.

Emails brought Anisha even closer to Sameer. So far, Anisha was infatuated with Sameer's personality. Sameer's way of speaking, his sense of humour, his way of loving had captivated Anisha's mind, but through the letters, Sameer's words invaded her heart from thousands of miles away.

Sometimes, Anisha and Sameer would chat for hours via the chat line on the computer. "Sameer, now Ashok's wedding is over, and you've got a job too. When are you getting married? Shall I introduce you to some American girl?" Anisha asked mischievously.

Sameer replied, "Why are you suggesting ruining another life? I am one of those people who, once committed, are committed forever."

It's April 16th today, Anisha's birthday. When Anisha opened her email in the morning after Rajiv left for work, Sameer's message was smiling at her on the screen with birthday wishes. Anisha's life had become encapsulated in that computer. She began to see electronic communication as the greatest gift of 1990s.

In America, Anisha didn't find the language in which romance could tickle her thoughts. Rajiv was a good person, for Anisha, he had as much time as a working man could spare for his wife. When they were together, their conversations didn't relate to their individual moods, neither did Rajiv have that language nor did Anisha have words to touch his heart.

In the evening, Rajiv returned with a gold chain for Anisha. But in her eyes, the weight of that chain was much lighter than Sameer's words.

One day, Sameer suddenly asked Anisha, "How did you spend your wedding night?"

Without hesitation, Anisha replied, "Thinking of you."

"Liar," Sameer wrote, "You must have spent the whole night in his arms, he must have touched you everywhere I once felt, and you tell me you were thinking of me."

"No, Sameer," Anisha began, her voice filled with seriousness, "Every waking moment, I've been lost in your thoughts. I've told you before, this heart belongs only to you and will always be forever yours."

Anisha knew she was speaking the truth, but she felt like Sameer did not believe her words.

A few days later, Rajiv informed Anisha that he had received her green card and could now visit India. Anisha's joy knew no bounds as she began preparations to go to Mumbai.

Upon hearing the news of her arrival, Sameer's excitement was boundless. Now he had his own flat in Kurla area of Mumbai. After his elder brother's marriage, the flat in Versova seemed small, so his father sold their village land and bought Sameer another flat.

The day arrived quickly, and Anisha found herself once again in Sameer's embrace.

Sameer's entire flat was adorned with colourful flowers. "After one and a half years, I am touching you! America seems to have agreed with you like a breath of fresh air," teased Sameer.

Anisha nestled in Sameer's arms, her voice trembling, "Keep quiet, just let me love you, I've been yearning for your kisses for a year and a half."

Anisha's lips and fingers had never teased Sameer like they did today. The contrast between the affections of an innocent maiden and a married woman one was beginning to crystallise for Sameer. Before, Anisha's hesitation, the shyness in her eyes, the trembling body that Sameer used to tease, no longer existed and today he was playing with her boldly and getting lost in her love with complete intoxication.

"It's getting late, aren't you going home, Anisha?" Sameer asked in surprise.

"Now I have a license, buddy, no fear at home. I'm married, and that too to an NRI, everyone at home is excited. I have already said I am going to meet old friends, will be back late," Anisha said boldly.

This saga continued for a month. Rajiv called every other day, but sometimes Anisha wouldn't even talk to him.

Today, when she met Sameer, she said, "Sameer, Rajiv called early in the morning today, and wants me to return."

"Hmm..." Sameer was just listening to Anisha.

"I spent the whole day worried. I don't want to go back to America anymore," Anisha said very seriously.

"Sameer, I want to live my life with you," Anisha said, with great conviction.

"Anisha, what are you saying? Don't be silly, are you thinking of leaving your husband? Who will let you do that?" Sameer said, surprised.

"Now I don't want to compromise my body, my life or my desires. I am fed up with this hypocrisy," Anisha retorted passionately.

Sameer sank into deep thought.

Breaking the silence, Anisha said, "My life is empty without you. All the glitz and glamour of America fades before your presence. The peace and pleasure I find in your arms is my heaven.

I want to leave everything, everything and come to you. I don't have the ability to sacrifice anymore. Sunaina is happy in her marital home. What my parents said, what they did, does that mean I have no right to live my life? Please... Sameer, I want to live a new life now, with you."

Anisha's words echoed in Sameer's ears all night. Today he had to make a decision. He loves Anisha with all his heart, but marriage, to a married woman! Some corner of his mind wasn't giving him permission for this. What will mom and dad think? *Bhabhi* (Sister-in-law) will ridicule me. Just a few days ago, when Ramu brought his new bride from the village, who looks just a little older than him, how much his *bhabhi* teased him! She even said directly to Ramu's face, 'Have she brought two or four children in dowry too?"

Meanwhile, Rajiv's phone call came early in the morning. "This house is empty without you. I've booked your ticket for day after tomorrow."

Anisha hung up the phone with exasperated tone, "Sorry Rajiv, I don't want to come back now. I'm divorcing you" and before Rajiv's phone could ring again, Anisha headed towards Sameer's flat.

Anisha embraced Sameer as soon as she saw him. Sameer also hugged her tightly. After a few moments of being embraced, Anisha said,

"Sameer, today I have come to you forever. Now I am entirely yours."

In response, Sameer said, "No, Anisha, this is not possible. I cannot accept you as a wife now. This does not mean that I don't love you. You are my first and only love. You are the most important chapter of my life, but as a lover, not as a wife."

Within split of a moment of Sameer's unacceptance, her world of love, emotions, and dedication crumbled to dust.

Women love only once...

In the serene surroundings of Hyde Park in London, by the edge of the Serpentine Lake Ram found himself seated on the same bench where Susan had once uttered those words, "Women love only once," as she gently crossed her legs while feeding the ducks. Ram's arms had once embraced her tightly.

Susan's statement had left Ram in a state of perplexity. If it were true, then how could Avantika have told Ram after their marriage that she loved her husband dearly, leading Ram to be forever estranged from her life? Did Avantika genuinely love her husband, or were those countless evenings spent with Ram during their college days just a passing phase? Or perhaps truth itself evolves with time, altering its principles and form?

The understanding that love could occur more than once in a lifetime dawned upon Ram that very day when Susan had kissed him upon his proposal. But today, Ram wished to delve deeper into this matter.

Lost in these thoughts, suddenly a smile crept onto Ram's lips, "Nonsense... it's all nonsense... these things are ephemeral." As Ram conversed with himself, he recalled the night when he had said "I love you" to the French call-girl in Paris and had lavished her with emotional words in the flow of passion. Yet, Susan had been the one he truly cherished. Every moment spent with her filled Ram with the utter happiness and love.

For the past three months, Susan's every evening had wrapped around Ram like the misty breeze of the Serpentine Lake.

Ram laid down on the same bench, and the moments spent with Susan began to replay in his mind like scenes from a movie.

"I love feeding the ducks... The name of this lake is Serpentine because it winds through Hyde Park like a snake... But I don't like this name... A snake is venomous, and this lake is sweet, very sweet... it adds sweetness to the entire Hyde Park... That's why when I get tired of dealing with customers at Marks & Spencer on Oxford Street all day long and crave some moments of peace, I come here before heading home... I love parks and rivers... Do you know, Ram? I often talk to these ducks... They've become my friends... I even feel excited to meet them on Sundays... It seems like if I don't show up, they'll remain hungry... And you're here too... Even if it's just for a few days... You'll remain a beautiful chapter in my life... I really like Indian people... I miss my childhood friends a lot... When my dad was posted at the British High Commission in Delhi, I was thirteen... I used to enjoy reading Hindi... Initially, I used to stammer, but gradually, I got the hang of it... I loved watching the Ramayana serial on TV... I often told my mom, get me married here in India... But Ram... my dream remained incomplete... Love happened with an Indian... but... let it be... I'll accept whatever fate has written for me on this earth..." A smile played on her lips, pearls of tears glistened in her eyes, and the warmth of love enveloped Susan in Ram's arms.

Suddenly, an ambulance or a police siren nearby broke Ram's reverie, and he sat up. Ram seemed troubled... Susan had been missing for two weeks now. Susan's phone was off, and the office informed him that she was on sick leave. Then her brother John informed Ram over the phone that "Susan is abroad." Ram had not met with Susan's family before, so he couldn't inquire further.

"Women love only once..." Susan's voice echoed in Ram's mind once again, and muttering to himself, Ram kicked a stone and headed towards his flat in Bayswater.

Nearby, in Bayswater, Ram's flat had been a love shack where he had felt the completeness of love in Susan's embrace many a times.

Just then, Ram's phone rang, and he heard his father's voice, "Ram... you've become a father, and I'm a grandfather... Radhika has given birth to a daughter."

Ram jumped with joy.

A few years later, it's December, the month of Christmas. The atmosphere in Manhattan, New York City, is bustling with people. This is the only festival where Europe and America seem immersed in joy once a year. Even the snow-covered evenings exude their full charm. Ram has come to New York to spend the holidays with his wife Radhika and their five-year-old daughter Ruchi.

"Mummy... who made the Statue of Liberty? Why is it in the middle of the ocean? Why do people rush so much here? If a fire breaks out in these tall buildings, what will happen?" Radhika was troubled by Ruchi's questions, so she said, "Go ask your dad."

"Dad, why do you walk so fast? Look, everyone here walks holding their wife's hand." Smiling, Ram, who was walking ahead, stopped and held Radhika's hand. "Happy now?" Ram said with a smile to Ruchi.

"No... both of you hold my hand... I'll walk in the middle." Ruchi held her parents' hands in hers.

Suddenly, Ram's steps halted in front of a Macy's store. Susan was standing at the bus stop. Unable to resist, Ram called out from behind, "Susan!"

"Hey, Ram..." Susan turned towards Ram with a smile.

"Hello Susan... Meet my wife Radhika... and this is Ruchi, my daughter." Susan greeted everyone with a smile.

Just then, an innocent face with messy hair behind Susan said, "And I'm Ricky... Susan's son."

Before the conversation could proceed further, the bus arrived at the stop, and Susan took her son's hand and boarded the bus.

Ram also hailed a taxi. As Radhika observed Ram's deep thoughts, she hesitantly asked, "Is she the same Susan you met in London?" Ram looked outside the taxi as he replied, "Yes."

Radhika didn't dare ask any further questions. She had seen Susan's son Ricky and had caught a glimpse of Ram's image in him. For a few moments, Radhika closed her eyes and prayed to her God, asking not to encounter another 'surprise' at a different turn.

"Women love only once..." Susan's words echoed once again in Ram's heart.

Dead End

In the playful waves of the Atlantic Ocean, Mini finds herself amidst the vastness of the sea, feeling the touch of destiny from afar, a destiny that is soon to unfold, a distance from her father, from her home, from her country. In three weeks, she'll be off to a boarding school in Switzerland where there will be new classmates but no father. Like a small boat sailing across the sea, Mini feels herself fading into the distance, going far away. She is going to be alone, far away from familiar roads, streets, parks, into new horizons.

In a moment, she turns her gaze to a joyful scene under a red and blue striped umbrella, Harsh was deeply involved in reading a novel, her father looks so alone to Mini. "No, my dad will be even more lonely without me," Mini says to herself as she takes a step towards her father.

The pages of joy are turning in the novel, but somewhere in his heart, Harsh feels disturbed. After Mini's departure, a desolate cave of loneliness appears before him in the clear light. After Sunaina's death, mornings and evenings held meaning in Harsh's life because of Mini, but how colourless will his life become after Mini's departure?

"Daddy..." Harsh realises from Mini's address that she has been staring at him intently for quite some time. Taking a sip of beer, Harsh puts his hand on Mini's hand and says, "Yes, dear."

"Daddy, please marry Aunt Julie," Mini begins.

Harsh, with a glass of beer in one hand, places the other hand on Mini and says, "That's not possible, dear. No one can replace your mom."

"Daddy, Aunt Julie is very nice. After I'm gone, she will take care of you completely," Mini tries to explain to her father.

Harsh realises that suddenly, thirteen-year-old Mini seems older than her age. He knows Mini is right. Julie was in love with Harsh all her life, hence her being single. She was Sunaina's good friend. She often took care of Mini post Sunaina's death. Raising a six-month-old child was very difficult, but it's hard for Harsh to understand that Julie, after marriage, would want her own child, which could bring various difficulties for Harsh and Mini's life.

Harsh tells Mini, "Dear, I could have married Julie many years ago, but your love means everything to me. I can't share your love with anyone else. I'm living just for you."

Kissing Mini's hands, Harsh continues, "My daughter is the best in the world. I don't have time for anyone else. I just want to be with you." Emptying the glass of beer, Harsh stands up.

With a slight smile on her lips, Mini says, "You know, Daddy, perhaps Mom didn't give you as much love as I did. You are the best daddy. But what will you do with your time now? I'm going to boarding school. I won't be able to chat with you on the internet all day long. How will you spend your time?"

Mini cleverly picks up on Harsh's words before he can say anything further. "You know, I really like Aunt Julie. I want her to stay with us. Actually, sometimes I get bored with you. You need girly friend at home. When I come home for holidays, there should be someone with whom I can have girly talks."

The emotional turmoil of separation and the bittersweetness of newfound responsibilities echo in their conversation, as Mini and Harsh navigate the complexities of their relationship and the uncertainties of the future.

Harsh couldn't help but chuckle at Mini's words. He smiled and said, "Alright, my dear, it's getting late. Can we talk about all this later? Give me some time, baby."

"Hmm... fair enough, but not too long, Dad," Mini giggled, picking up her bag and heading towards the car with Harsh.

Exhausted from the day's events, Mini sank into a deep sleep as soon as she reached home. But the turmoil in Harsh's mind kept the tranquillity of sleep from settling in so easily. Harsh too wished that Julie become his life partner. After Sunaina's death, it was Julie who provided support the heartbroken Harsh and Mini. It took Harsh three years to recover from Sunaina's death. He still remembers vividly the night of Mini's third birthday when, at Mini's insistence, Julie had to stay overnight at Harsh's house, and that night, a physical relationship developed between the two. Harsh often wonders what that meant and why was Julie oblivious to his pain after he was with her. Their relationship was not fleeting, otherwise, a broken Harsh wouldn't have been transformed into a confident and successful businessman.

But marriage to Julie...? That question always troubled Harsh. Julie was everything that a good wife and a mother who loved Mini should be. But Julie's desire to become a mother herself was a big obstacle for Harsh in accepting her as his wife. He always feared that the arrival of another child in the family might bring uncertainty to Mini. He didn't want to hurt Julie because of his love for Mini.

Suddenly, the phone rang. Harsh knows it's Julie's call. She calls every night to say goodnight.

"How was your day, Harsh? Did Mini enjoy herself?" Julie's voice seems to offer solace to Harsh's restlessness once again.

"It was wonderful, Julie. I was just thinking about you," Harsh replied.

"No need to say it, darling. I'm aware of your thoughts. I've kept track of your heartbeat," Julie said, laughing.

Harsh also lit a cigarette with a smile. Julie may be English, but she understands Indian thoughts and conversations perfectly.

"Your words make me melt, Julie," Harsh replied.

Julie continued, "Okay... now tell me, what were you thinking?"

"Nothing special... just about you... waiting for your call," Harsh said.

Julie laughed, "So, sir, are you still afraid of getting married?"

Harsh was taken aback. "What do you mean?" Julie remained silent for a moment. Harsh began to understand everything. "Okay, so this is Mini's and your conspiracy!"

"Harsh dear... yes... now don't take me wrong, please," Julie began to clarify her side. "Actually, it was Mini who brought it up yesterday when she visited my boutique. I was really surprised for a moment. You know, Harsh, Mini is no longer a child. Today's children are smarter than us."

The conversation between Harsh and Julie reflected the emotional complexities of their relationship as well as the evolving dynamics between Harsh, Mini, and Julie; navigating the delicate balance between love, responsibility, and the desire for companionship.

Harsh, speaking with gravity, said, "But Julie... my problem is a bit different. You know that your dream is to have your own child. And even if I were to agree to that, will Mini be able to accept it?"

Despite the seriousness in Harsh's words, Julie just laughed and said, "Go and speak to your daughter, you silly man... Good night."

Deep in thought, Harsh took the last drag of his cigarette and extinguished the remaining butt in the ashtray. Today, for the first time, Harsh felt that he could give a child a mother's love, but he couldn't become a grown girl's friend. The friendship between Julie and Mini was giving him immense happiness today. But another child in the family, Mini's stepbrother or stepsister... no, Mini would not accept it. Harsh struggled with his thoughts until he finally drifted off to sleep.

The morning rays of the sun knocked on Harsh's eyes. As he reached the shower, he found himself engulfed in the same dilemma as last night. But there was no resolution. The problem remained the same, the question lingered: will Mini accept his second child?

In the living room, Mini, dressed in a red t-shirt and a yellow skirt, flicked through TV channels with the remote in her hand, lost in search of her favourite program, perhaps awaiting Harsh's presence. As she saw Harsh, she said, "Good morning, Daddy."

Harsh approached her, kissing her forehead, and said, "Good morning, darling. Let's have breakfast."

Both father and daughter had breakfast in silence, as if they were waiting to hear something from each other. Breaking the silence, Mini said, "Daddy, when will you take me shopping for Switzerland? It's been two weeks since the school sent the complete list. Shall I ring, Auntie Julie?"

Harsh's serious face turned into a smile. He understood that Mini was back on the same topic. He secretly wished for it too.

"No, not at all... you don't have to bother her for every small thing. I'll take you shopping," Harsh said, taking the last sip of tea.

Now Mini's patience seemed to be wearing thin. She said, "Daddy... you know what I mean?" As she said this, Mini came behind Harsh and put her hand lovingly on his shoulder, saying, "Dad... can I say something? I want a baby brother."

Harsh moved her hand away, standing up, and said, "You're talking too much. You're not big enough yet to understand everything."

The truth was that Mini was giving Harsh everything without even asking. Looking at Mini's drooping face, Harsh held her hand and said, "Okay, dear, I'll talk to Julie."

In a flash, Mini's happiness returned to her face. Harsh felt proud of his daughter. He was amazed at how much maturity had come into Mini's understanding. From being a playful child in his arms until yesterday, today Mini was planning her father's life with the colours of the rainbow.

A week before Mini's departure for Switzerland, Harsh and Julie tied knot. A week of laughter and playfulness passed in Mini's packing, Julie's advice to her, and so on.

"Tomorrow morning, you are going to take your first step towards your future, Mini. Daddy won't be there to wake you up in the morning or tuck you in at night. You'll have to take care of yourself," Harsh said, his eyes moistening as he spoke.

Mini, placing her hand on Harsh's cheeks, said, "I am no longer a kid, Dad. I am your responsible daughter; I can take care of myself. The alarm of your clock, your picture to find solace in, I'll try to find lullabies in your memories. But I will really miss you, Dad. Mom's dream was for me to study in Switzerland, and the time has come to fulfil that dream. Your teachings and Mom's dream are my greatest strengths, Dad."

As Mini spoke, she couldn't stop herself and began to cry, resting her head on Harsh's lap.

Farewells are always like this. On one side, the desire for a golden future, on the other, the pain of separation from loved ones. Who can escape the cycle of time? Harsh kept gazing at the departing plane until it disappeared from sight.

Meanwhile, Mini got busy in her new school, in a new world with new friends. And here, Harsh and Julie started flowing in the stream of married life. Christmas time is extremely busy for both Harsh and Julie. The crowd of shoppers in Julie's boutique and the late-night opening of Harsh's supermarket, Mini decided not to come to London during the holidays, understanding this reality.

Harsh and Julie are happy together. They sit openly with friends and relatives. Visiting people's homes and having guests over, everything has become a beautiful part of life.

January 1st, New Year... With the first rays of sun, Julie writes her request on Harsh's lips, which Harsh gladly accepts, cuddling Julie in his arms. Seeing a new glow in Julie's eyes and feeling it, Harsh asks, "What do you want, a son or a daughter?"

Resting her head on Harsh's shoulders, a slightly embarrassed Julie says, "Dear! We already have a daughter."

Harsh smiles and kisses Julie's forehead. Julie starts saying, "You know Harsh, I have always had a great desire for children since the age of sixteen. When I used to ask my mother when would I have a baby, she always used to laugh and say, 'When you become old, and I always used to wait for her to become old.' When you came into my life, I don't know why, but I started nurturing the desire to become a mother to your child."

Harsh saw a sixteen-year-old girl in Julie's words. Playing with Julie's hair, he says, "I am aware of your desire, Julie. Just because of Mini... You know how much I love Mini. Maybe I took time in understanding your desires."

Harsh and Julie now start spending time awaiting this new dream. But even after six months, when Julie didn't conceive, one day they both decided to seek advice from a doctor. The doctor took some tests and asked them to come next Monday for her results and advice.

Meanwhile, Mini eagerly awaits her return home during the summer vacation in Switzerland. Mini tells her best friend Suzie, "Ten months have passed, but this last week before the holidays doesn't seem to pass. I feel like going home soon."

Suzie says, "Don't worry, Mini, you are no longer a kid. Our school group is going to America. It will be a great fun. Come with us for a month, then spend the rest of the time at home."

Mini said angrily, "Don't be silly, Suzie! My dad will kill me. You don't know how much he loves me. America... that's a distant dream. He won't even let me out of his sight for a moment during the holidays."

"Okay, okay, Daddy's baby, I'm sorry," Suzie said, placing her hand on Mini's shoulder.

"You reminded me of Dad, Suzie. Let's go and call him now," Mini said while dialling Harsh's number, teasingly adding, "Dad, can I go to America with my friends from school? It's just for a month, I'll spend the rest of the time with you."

Interrupting her, Harsh said, "Shut up! If you say anything more, I'll cancel your education in Switzerland and call you back."

Mini burst out laughing on the phone.

Surprised, Suzie asked Mini, "What's this, Mini? You just said you won't go to America, and now you're talking to Daddy like this?"

Laughing, Mini replied, "I was just teasing Dad. I can't live without him."

On Monday morning, as they were leaving the house, Julie reminded Harsh that they had to go to the doctor today. Harsh said, "I shall go directly there, Julie. I'll bring the report and come straight to your boutique."

In a short while, Harsh was sitting in front of the doctor.

The doctor said to Harsh, "Harsh... I'm really sorry to say, you can never become a father. Your body doesn't have the seeds required to become a father and is infertile."

Harsh felt like the ground was slipping beneath his feet. Darkness engulfed him for a moment.

He said, "But Doctor... I already have a daughter."

The doctor replied, "I'm sorry again, Harsh. She may not be yours."

Harsh's jaw dropped in shock! he felt like he was being hit blow after blow. A storm seemed to have entered his life unexpectedly.

With heavy feet dragging the ground, Harsh moved towards his car. In a moment, everything changed. What he had been living for Sunaina and Mini, all of that seemed a betrayal. Sunaina's affair with someone else and Mini, an illegitimate child... the flood of emotions played a cruel joke. Such a painful violation of trust and love?

Harsh sat in the car, not knowing where to go. He couldn't see any path ahead. Just then, Harsh's phone rang, seeing Mini's number on the screen, he pressed the red button to end the call and started grappling with his emotions. All the love, trust, and dedication of a lifetime shattered before him. On the other hand, Julie... what would Harsh say to her? He could never fulfil Julie's biggest and most important dream. His body was just a facade. He was not worthy of Julie. The internal conflict and the erupting volcano in his mind were becoming uncontrollable. A turmoil that seemed to have come into his life to never be silent again.

One reasoning after another... Harsh was struggling with himself as he was dealing with the onslaught of the past; the golden future was drowning in the darkness of dilemma. Harsh felt like he had fallen from the sky today... in such a situation, every element of nature turned away from him to provide any support. "Mini -whom I loved more than life itself, is not my daughter. Sunaina - whom I thought understood the meaning of trust and love, is someone else's child's mother. And ultimately, Julie - who had been choking on her desires for a long time for me and our child; I am not worthy of her." The net of dilemma and despair was entangling Harsh more and more.

The betrayal and immorality of Sunaina's breach of trust left Harsh bleeding emotionally, but he didn't want to cause havoc in Julie's life. Mini's innocent face adorned with a stranger's image; this truth was slowly transforming Harsh's pride into ego. Every heartbeat began to feel like a burden. In the dark and deep abyss of emptiness, Harsh kept stumbling. Rejecting his fate, a crumbling Harsh began searching for a decision within himself.

A few moments later, Mini's phone rang again. Harsh, after some thought, answered, "Hello..."

In a mischievous tone, Mini said, "Dad, I'm thinking of going to America with my friends."

In a very serious tone, Harsh replied, "That's okay, you can go."

Before Mini could say anything else, Harsh hung up the phone.

Starting the car, Harsh didn't know which way to go. It seemed like he had forgotten the way back home today.

Suddenly, he saw a red signboard and slammed on the brakes, on which was written 'Dead End'.

The Wait

At the crack of dawn, Deepak is in a hurry, rushing through every task. Often the one to arrive at the office by 10, Deepak is there today by quarter to nine. The one who never refuses attending any meeting, Deepak has postponed two meetings today. His secretary Rosy couldn't help but notice. Around noon, she asked Deepak, "Deepak, you seem to be in a hurry today and also glowing. What's going on?"

With a smile, Deepak first said, "Nothing..." then continued, "Today is the fifth anniversary of my marriage, I'm planning a surprise for Shalini."

Rosy was struck by Deepak's words. Such happiness on their wedding anniversary? This thought didn't leave Rosy's mind. She had been working with Deepak for the past three years, and she had never seen him like this before. Never had she seen such eagerness in Deepak, neither on any other wedding anniversary nor on Deepak's or Shalini's birthdays. In fact, among colleagues and friends around Deepak, there had always been talks that Deepak was not happy with his marriage. There could be a separation between them at any time.

Rosy wondered what was going on in her mind. She came to her desk and started looking at the appointment calendar for the past years on her computer. On March 21, 2005, last year, Deepak had left the office at eight in the evening, taking some buyers from France out to dinner. March 21, 2004, was a Sunday, but at that time, Deepak was not in the country; he was in California at a garment exhibition. So, what's special this year?

Just then, Rosy's phone rang. From the other end, Deepak was saying, "Rosy, can you order a romantic strawberry-flavoured cake for me? Please... I've never bought cakes before... so I'm asking you... you are very sweet."

"Sure, Deepak..." Rosy replied, her dilemma growing. Anyway... Rosy obeyed her boss and ordered the cake.

Lost in thought, Rosy first tried to convince herself, "I'm also crazy, why am I so worried about Deepak? It's his life." Then she couldn't stop her eagerness and picked up the phone, meeting Deepak in his cabin, saying, "Sir, the cake will be ready at Peter's Bakery by five. Shall I pick it up myself or...?"

Cutting her off, Deepak said, "No... no... don't worry... I'll pick it up on my way home."

As Rosy continued, "Anything else...like a bouquet or a dinner table somewhere..." Deepak silenced her, saying, "No thanks Rosy... leave that to me."

Deepak silenced Rosy, but his mind was preoccupied.

Last year, he had reached home at midnight on his wedding anniversary. Shalini, knowing that Deepak was coming late, had decorated the house with candles and prepared Chinese food with her own hands, waiting for Deepak's arrival.

Deepak had just said to Shalini as he entered the room, "I've told you so many times not to wait for me. This is my life. Never wait for me."

But today... today Deepak is in a different mood. He wants to correct his mistakes. He wants to wash away all the insults he has hurled at Shalini's love. Deepak, who hadn't really embraced Shalini from the first day of their marriage, now wants to give Shalini all the happiness.

This change came to Deepak in just a few months. He had become humble towards Shalini. Although he forced Shalini to get a job, he now didn't like Shalini working outside.

Shalini had come from a small town in India to London, and Deepak was born in London itself. Deepak had married Shalini with his family's consent. It's not that his family had forced him to marry Shalini, but at that time, Deepak didn't take his marriage seriously.

Deepak had been in love with Anjali since he was 17. Anjali also studied in the same school as him and she too loved him. The love affair between Anjali and Deepak lasted for seven years, then one day suddenly Anjali told Deepak that she was marrying a doctor from Canada.

Deepak felt like a mountain of sorrow had collapsed on him that day. He tried to convince Anjali, but Anjali only said that life doesn't survive on just love. At that time, Deepak had completed his MBA and had just started his new job. Anjali had chosen a respectable and wealthy doctor in Canada as her life partner. Anjali was also from a wealthy family. She didn't want to live in a small flat with Deepak.

Anjali had told Deepak at that time that she had always seen him as just a boyfriend, not as a husband. In her eyes, Deepak could be a good friend but nothing more, not even a husband.

Deepak was stunned by Anjali's thoughts. He had never thought of anyone else in his life other than Anjali.

After Anjali's marriage, Deepak wandered around like a madman for about a year. Then after the persuasion of his family members, he married Shalini. But Shalini was not his love. He couldn't separate himself emotionally from Anjali.

Shalini was a girl who remained silent. Despite being understanding, she never complained about anything to Deepak. Deepak never mistreated Shalini. He always conducted himself with politeness, but the only thing missing was love.

Deepak, despite wanting to, couldn't include Shalini in his heart. Their physical relationship was also pure formality. Deepak understood that he couldn't give Shalini any happiness, but he was helpless from his heart. Even though he wanted to, he couldn't connect with Shalini. He couldn't remove Anjali's image from his mind. Deepak and Shalini were together, but there was an invisible emptiness in their lives. Besides the void of love and romance, there was also a communication gap between them. They only talked about work. There was nothing more in their relationship.

So, what happened to make Deepak fall so deeply in love with Shalini? Today, Shalini is the only one residing in Deepak's heart.

Shalini was a girl of extremely graceful nature, just like her name denotes. She silently tried to win Deepak's love many times. Sometimes she would bake a cake with her own hands on Deepak's birthday, and sometimes she would decorate the house with flowers in anticipation of Deepak's arrival. Two years ago, when Deepak was in America on his wedding anniversary, Shalini had sent him a beautiful card handmade from London via courier, but Deepak had ignored that card too.

Shalini continued to endure such mental neglect, but she didn't raise her voice. If someone knew about Shalini's sad feelings, it was Rajesh. Rajesh worked with Shalini in her office. By sharing her sorrow with Rajesh, Shalini would lighten her heart.

Three months ago, while returning from a Christmas party, Deepak had an accident. He fractured his leg, which forced him to stay home for two months. He would stay alone at home all day and become bored. When Shalini came back home after work, it felt like brightness had entered their home.

Deepak missed Shalini the most on New Year's Eve when Shalini didn't come home all night and was busy at her office party. At that time, Deepak couldn't say anything to Shalini because he had never spent a New Year's Eve with Shalini before, and also, Shalini's busy schedule in such events had become a part of her work.

This was the first time in Deepak's life that he couldn't sleep all night and kept waiting for Shalini. When Shalini arrived home at five in the morning, for the first time, she looked extremely beautiful in a black cut top, skirt, and a red belt. Perhaps Deepak had never noticed Shalini before. It was the moment when Deepak felt envious seeing Shalini in such an attire for the first time.

For the past three months, Deepak had been thinking about Shalini, but he didn't get the chance to express himself, nor did he find the courage. Once, he asked Shalini to go to dinner, but Shalini refused. Deepak didn't insist much because he felt that Shalini had now developed a habit of staying away from him, and to become close to Shalini, he would have to change himself.

Today, on March 21, 2006, on their fifth wedding anniversary, Deepak chose to express his feelings to Shalini. Now, Deepak feels that Anjali is his past and Shalini is his future. Today, he dreams of shaping his future together.

As soon as he left the office, Deepak first picked the cake and then stopped at a flower shop. He bought all the orchids in the shop. Shalini liked orchids very much. She often decorated the house with these flowers.

Deepak is very happy. He knows that Shalini must have prepared some special dish of his liking today and must be waiting for him eagerly.

Deepak is thinking about how happy Shalini will be to see all this. Today, he will first ask for forgiveness for his mistakes and then will kiss her lips as if to make up for everything.

On the way, Deepak also bought some new music CDs and a gift for Shalini.

Upon reaching home, Deepak first went to the door and rang the bell, then suddenly, he took out the key from his pocket and quietly opened the door. He wanted to surprise Shalini.

The house was empty; Shalini was nowhere to be seen. For a moment, Deepak felt anxious, then quickly, with a smile, he started arranging the orchids.

"It seems like Shalini is upstairs in the room. I will quickly set up the lounge; it will be so much fun," he said to himself while lighting candles.

Then Deepak had an idea. He turned on the music player, put a new CD in it, and quietly hid behind the door of the lounge.

Today, Deepak's mind is jumping like that of a teenage boy. He feels like he is sixteen or seventeen years old.

About ten minutes passed, but still, Shalini didn't come downstairs. Deepak felt a little worried and went upstairs to the room.

The room was dark. Deepak switched the light on, but Shalini was not there. Deepak peeked into the bathroom, but Shalini was not there either.

Then Deepak noticed an envelope near the bed with "To Deepak..." written on it.

Deepak picked up the envelope and started reading the letter inside.

The letter read:

"Dear Deepak,

I waited for five long years, but you never came. Neither did I ever ask you for the reason, nor did you ever say anything to me. I don't want to be a burden in your life anymore.

I'm leaving your life forever and eloping with Rajesh.

Be happy always.

Shalini."

Dilemma

It's two o' clock in the night. Chandini's flight to Mumbai is scheduled at 11 in the morning. Heathrow airport in London is just 10 miles away from Sagar's flat. Chandni, with a light shawl over her head, contemplates. It seems she has to take a taxi in the morning since Sagar had a bit too much to drink. Moments of silence linger. Chandni's hand reaches for the TV remote. Sagar grabs Chandni's hand, "Please! I just want to spend these moments with you before you leave. You'll be gone by morning. I know ten days isn't much time, but even in the past eleven months, not a moment has passed without you, and your leaving weighs heavily on my heart."

Chandni smiles, kissing Sagar's hand, "And what about when you went to America for a week? Don't you remember? You don't know how I spent that time."

"I know, my darling. That trip of mine began your journey of poetry writing inspired by my paintings. You truly have made my paintings come alive," Sagar says, pressing Chandni's fingers.

Chandni becomes a bit serious, "Leave it, Sagar. Just remember the person you have painted for. Just remember her. I am only a..."

Interrupting, Sagar stops Chandni, "There may be traces of Asmita in them, but she never found time to see or try to understand these paintings. She had no interest in paintings, but you, Chand, the way you look at each stroke, the figures on these canvases, feel them, it seems like they were created just for you."

"No," Chandni says, "My creation is due to your paintings. Each stroke denotes and exudes dedication to your craft. But Sagar," Chandni says with some surprise, "Has Asmita never mentioned or commented on your paintings?"

Looking dejected, Sagar replied, "Nothing like that comes to mind. But I'm not worried. Asmita was the inspiration for my paintings. Her coming into my life is the reason for this art."

"Do you love her a lot, Sagar?" Chandni asks, teasing Sagar's chest with her fingertips, "Your paintings before and after Asmita's marriage show your emotions like a mirror to me. I like it."

Resting her head on Sagar's chest, Chandni continues, "I love capturing every emotion of yours. I love being close to you... and bringing you closer."

"I know, Chand," Sagar says, caressing Chandni's cheeks with his hands, "I don't know how, but I've laid every page of my life open in front of you. More than that, whenever Asmita's thoughts come to my mind, I immediately tell you. You also..."

"I know, Chand!" Sagar interrupts, "The foundation of our relationship is honesty and truth. Do you remember... What brought us close to each other? Your feelings penned down inspired by the strokes of my brush was a melting point of two hearts. Your coming to the Nehru Centre for my painting exhibition became the greatest blessing of my life."

Sagar begins to dive into memories, "Remember, Chandni, as soon as I mentioned calling a taxi, you proposed helping me deliver the paintings to my house. I am very reserved by nature, but I don't know what charm was in your proposal that I said yes at once."

Chandni's intoxication with Sagar's words deepens, "Then over coffee, you kept me engaged in conversations all night long... No... no, sweetheart, I willingly kept flowing in your ocean of art, and I never want to stop this flow."

"Don't even try, Chand. Just as my past love gave birth to this art, it will die without your fragrance in my life. Today, my sketches are shaped by your verses. My brush awaits your poetry on canvas. The day this wait ends, my strokes will end. Sagar says looking deep into her eyes.

"No... no, Sagar, that should never happen," Chandni says, suddenly sitting up. "You know I have no destination. I have pledged never to marry after my sister Rajni's death, and I told you this on the first day. My whole life is laid out before you, Sagar. You have to settle somewhere. I am a companion to your life who, even though not present, will always be with you."

Sagar gazes towards Chandni with melancholy. Speaking as if searching for words, he says, "I know Anu, Rajni's daughter and her responsibilities lie with you. I am here with you, with every thought of yours. Being a good friend and lover, fulfilling my duty is my desire. I can't think of anything else other than you. I am yours every moment, every hour, dwelling in your thoughts. I long to spend my life immersed in those moments when you are with me."

"What kind of love is yours, Sagar? On one hand, a corner of your heart is a prisoner of Asmita's, and on the other, you have captured me so strongly in your emotions " Chandni questions.

Sagar, lost in Chandni's eyes, says, "I want to respect every relationship in life. Someone's entry into life and making their place could be a coincidence, but for me, the significance of that place in my heart is never lessened by anyone else's arrival. I never want to be so weak that I forget the friendship of bygone moments."

Sagar's hand moves towards the packet of cigarettes. Chandni extends her hand to help him. As Sagar lights his cigarette, he continues, "It is true that Asmita's father should have been welcomed into the family, and my ego couldn't accept that. Asmita couldn't leave her family, and I couldn't leave my ideals. But disrespecting the emotions, the moments of love that I have felt, would be a dishonour. And... it would be disrespectful to our relationship if I keep something different in my heart and something else on my lips." Sagar holds Chandni in his embrace, continuing, "Chandni, you are my today, and I am yours. Let's make our present golden. Let no shadow of constraint fall on the height of our love. Life is to be lived, and we shall live it with complete freedom, with complete respect and with complete love."

"If your heart wanders to someone else," Chandni says, nestled in Sagar's arms, "then..."

"I will tell you first," Sagar interrupts, smiling.

"Move aside, rascal," Chandni says, pushing Sagar lightly.

"My Chand," Sagar says, turning serious again, "Look, both of us are engaged in our own pursuits. We meet so many people every day. You run a promotion company, dealing with new artists; in a way, you are in the show business, and I also work in an import-export company alongside being an artist. It's natural to often be attracted to others and make friends with those we like. Rising above hypocrisy is our shared belief, but yes, it would be wrong to disrespect each other's emotions and love."

"One minute... one minute..." Chandni interjects, "Let's shed some light on this freedom."

With a smile, Sagar removes the ash from his cigarette and says, "What's wrong with making friends with someone you like, establishing new relationships? Yes, it would be wrong if we forget each other's relationships, love and trust. We always have to respect each other's emotions."

Agreeing with Sagar's perspective, Chandni gently places her lips on his forehead. After a few moments of silence, Sagar says, "Let's go,

Chand... it's already seven in the morning, let's get ready to leave."

Sagar continued to gaze at Chandni until she faded from his sight at the departure terminal and turned towards home with tears in his eyes. He painted a picture of Chandni for the first time. The scene of Chandni disappearing from his sight was captured on his canvas.

The conversation between Sagar and Chandni continued over the phone. Time seemed to slow down for Sagar for the first time in his life. Two days before Chandni's return to London, Sagar called her, "Hey Chand," to which the response came, "Hey Sagar... I'll call you back, I'm a bit busy."

Sagar said okay and hung up. Today, Sagar is excited to tell Chandni that he has painted her picture. The whole evening passed, and Chandni didn't call. Sagar became worried. He tried calling Chandni several times, but she wasn't in her hotel room.

As the night progressed, Sagar called again, thinking that it must be around 2 in the morning in India, and Chandni must surely be in her room. His thoughts proved true; as soon as he heard Chandni's voice, Sagar leaped with joy, "Chand... where are you...?"

From the other end, Chandni replied, "Sorry Sagar... I'm very tired and fell asleep as soon as I got to the hotel... Let's talk in the morning." Chandni hung up without saying goodbye.

Sagar wasn't feeling good. Yet, he found himself lost in those beautiful moments he had spent in Chandni's embrace.

The wait was over as Sagar arrived at the airport with a bouquet of flowers, including yellow ones that Chandni adored.

As soon as they got in the car, Chandni said, "Take me to Victoria Station, I urgently need to go to Southampton."

Sagar was surprised and asked Chand if she was, okay? "Do you know what I've prepared for your welcome at home? It's your picture, the one you've been waiting for a long time". Sagar used to say that he didn't need to raise his brush to make the picture, it would form by itself. "I have been feeling something new in my heart these last few days, resulting in your picture. I don't use my hands to paint, I use my heart to add colour to my paintings."

Chandni smiled, albeit without much enthusiasm, and said, "That's your profession, but I need to go home now. Anu is not feeling well, and I must go home."

"What happened to Anu?" Sagar asked, surprised.

"Nothing, just a flu. Please drop me at the closest station and I'll take the train," Chandni replied casually. Sagar's insistence to drop her at Southampton was also refused.

Sagar kept getting more and more disheartened. Still, he reasoned with himself that Chandni had come from India, tired and troubled, which might have caused some changes in her behaviour. Sagar's heart suddenly felt a pang when Chandni got off at the station, leaving the flowers he gave her in the car.

Sagar felt his home was suffocating him, like a train had run over his dreams. Chandni's picture began to seem more lifelike to him. He sat on the armchair lost deeply in thoughts.

Sometime later, the phone rang. "Hello Sagar", Chandni's voice made Sagar happy and alive. "Sorry, the flowers stayed in the car." "I will come soon and see the picture you painted."

Sagar started feeling happy again. Sagar and Chandni kept talking again on the phone for a few days. However, Sagar felt something was missing.

Almost a week later, Sagar expressed his desire to meet Chandni, which she welcomed. He started driving towards Southampton.

They chatted while sitting in the lawn for some time, then Chandni got up to make tea inside. Sagar's gaze fell on Chandni's mobile, where a message flashed on the screen. Sagar picked up the phone and read, "Sweetheart, you stole my sleep."

Sagar was stunned. His whole life seemed to halt. Meanwhile, Anu came inside. Sagar, unable to bear it anymore, left without saying anything.

Outside, Chandni couldn't find Sagar and started getting worried. She began calling on Sagar's mobile, but in vain... it was switched off. Chandni started feeling restless. Unable to stay, she too drove towards London.

Meanwhile, lost in deep thoughts and swallowing the pain, Sagar arrived home. All the pictures of his life were swirling before him; Chandni's promises echoed in his ears. He made a decision, lit a cigarette, and started sipping the pain on the armchair. Suddenly, the doorbell rang... he opened the door. Chandni was standing in front of him.

Sagar sarcastically remarked, "Surprised how you managed to follow me?"

"Sagar," Chandni said, "You should have been surprised if I didn't follow you, especially in a way you left without telling me."

Sagar remained silent and continued the conversation, "Chand, has someone else entered your life?"

After a moment of silence, Chandni replied, "No, that's your illusion. You're too suspicious."

Sagar responded, "I'm walking on the path of truth, so I said what was in my heart."

Chandni also said in response, "Never change your path, Sagar. Your path is the power of love."

"And you, Chand?" Sagar interrupted, showing him her disappearing picture, "Every picture has been a dream of my life. Look, this is the reality of my life."

Tears welled up in Chandni's eyes as she spoke, "No matter what happens, I won't leave your life, nor will I let you go."

"But, am I not your future, Chand?" Sagar questioned.

Grasping Sagar's shirt, Chandni replied, "But you are my present, and you will always be."

Sagar found himself in a strange dilemma, unsure of what to say. He took a deep breath and finished his drink in one gulp. Retreating his hand from Chandni's grip, he sat back in his armchair. Chandni, sitting on the sofa, rested her head on Sagar's knees and said, "Sagar, I'm searching for myself. Who am I? What am I? Why am I? My character, my existence, what are they? I've been distancing myself from myself these past few days. Sometimes, I just want to be alone. Maybe that's why, knowingly or unknowingly, I'm hurting you. You're my closest friend. It's essential for me to have you in my life. I can't bear to see you upset. I'm sorry, Sagar, for everything."

Sagar remained silent, his eyes closed, absorbing Chandni's words. Her nails started digging into Sagar's feet, and she nestled closer to him. Sagar, feeling the pain, struggled to break his silence, "Chand, isn't it true that you made an excuse for Anu's illness? Isn't it true that someone else has entered your life lately? Isn't it true that you're deceiving me with lies?"

Before Chandni could respond, Sagar interrupted, placing his hand on Chandni's cheek, "Chand, it's not wrong for someone else to enter our lives, welcoming beloved companions into our lives isn't a sin. Breaking ties with past happiness for the arrival of new joys isn't wrong either. I'm with you and will continue to be, as long as you're with me."

Chandni suddenly broke down into tears, sobbing uncontrollably.

Brushing her forehead with his lips, Sagar said, "I welcome your new companion. I love everyone who loves you. Because I truly love you. I can't even think of anything bad about you."

After a moment of silence, Chandni spoke, "Yes... it's true. I met Aman. He's an emerging singer from Mumbai, and his voice is unique. But more than his talent, I got drawn to his personality, his character, the influence of his words. He has everything that attracts me."

Sagar's heart was wounded by Chandni's words, but he contained his pain within a lovingly solemn expression as he gently ran his fingers through Chandni's hair, silently absorbing her words.

Chandni continued, "For the first time, I'm sinking into a whirlpool where drowning is the only option. I'm not holding back. Aman's entry into my life, the impact on my emotions, I didn't even realise when your thoughts didn't cross my mind, and I got lost in his flow. What should I do, Sagar? What should I do? I know the foundation of our relationship is truth, and yet, I've become its enemy. I'm sorry, Sagar."

Sagar embraced Chandni tightly, saying, "It's okay, Chand. For your happiness, I'll stay in your life just like a friend. This is the test of our love, and I believe I will pass such tests."

After a few moments, Sagar said, "Chand, it is getting late. If you have to go, leave now; otherwise, stay here."

In response, Chandni said, "No, Sagar, Anu is alone at home. I have to go, and it's not a lie. Today, it feels like the burden of these past few days has been lifted off my shoulders. Thank you, Sagar. You're my saviour. Your heart is like your name, vast like an ocean. You're a golden chapter in my life. I won't let your paintings stop."

Taking Chandni's hand, Sagar said, "No, Chand, whether my paintings continue or not, I can't promise. But I'll always be in your life, painting or not."

"No, no, you will definitely continue painting, Sagar. I won't let your paintings stop," Chandni vehemently opposed Sagar's statement.

Not escalating the argument further, Sagar said, "Chand, it's getting late; you should leave now."

Looking at the clock, Chandni said, "Yes, Sagar, it's getting late. I have to go. Thank you."

On one hand Sagar is accepting Chandni given the circumstances. On the other hand, Chandni is captivated by Aman's personality. Whilst travelling on the motorway from London to Southampton, In the turmoil of conflicting emotions, Chandni's mobile rang, "Hello, Aman here, my sweetheart... Why were you silent all day? Are you okay?"

"Yes, Aman, I was with Sagar the whole time. He found out about us," Chandni began sharing her pain with Aman, the floodgates of her heart now open.

Oh... Did he confront you? Are you alright? What was your response to him? He bombarded her with a barrage of questions.

Chandni responds emotionally, "No.. no.. Aman, Sagar was so nice to me. He accepted our relationship and even forgave me. He wants to meet you too."

Aman, surprised, exclaimed, "Really.. How close were you two.. I mean, did you…?"

Chandni didn't like Aman's overtones, she said, "I don't know what the definition of physical intimacy is in your eyes, but in mine, the answer to your question is 'yes.' I was with Sagar, with my body and soul today."

The voice on the phone sounded a bit strained. Aman interrupted the conversation, saying, "Okay.. let's talk tomorrow. Good night, Chandni."

As soon as she reached home, Chandni called Sagar, "Hey Sagar, how are you now?"

"Alone," Sagar replied in one word.

"Never, as long as I'm alive... Be warned never to say such a thing," Chandni expressed her disagreement with Sagar's thoughts.

Sagar changed the subject, "And tell me, Chand... how are you? What are your plans for the future with Aman? Let me know if I can help in any way."

"Sagar," Chandni said, "Talk to me about yourself.. I don't know where my life will take me. I don't even know myself."

"That's what I'm talking about," Sagar began, "You are my life."

"Hey.. Sagar.. I'm enthralled by your words. Tell me one thing... Can a person love two people at the same time?" Chandni asked.

"Yes, absolutely," Sagar replied, "If they have the strength to step on two boats, they can do anything with two people at the same time."

Chandni argued, "But a boat moves with just two oars, right?"

"Chand," Sagar intervened, "Who wins in a dialogue with a writer? I think it's time to leave fate to its course."

Chandni laughed.

The night passed with all three tangled in emotions. Sagar, Chandni, and Aman, victims of both time and emotions.

In the morning, Chandni called Aman in Mumbai, "Hello Aman.. Good morning."

"Good morning, Chandni.. Missing you badly.. You've created a huge vacuum in my life. Please come back," Aman expressed his love to Chandni.

"I'm in a dilemma, Aman. I couldn't see Sagar's condition yesterday. His paintings, his inspiration, his life resonates with my name alone. He has become the definition of love in my life, the kind that's only found in books," Chandni poured her feelings to Aman.

"Yes, Chandni.. You're right.. I've come between you two.. Just stay happy. That's my wish...I can spend my whole life in your memory, or let's say.. those two days you gave me mean a lot to me, just don't worry," Aman expressed his devotion to Chandni.

"No.. Aman, I can't leave either of you. But it's also true that with my desire, I'll only bring you both pain," Chandni expressed her dilemma to Aman, "My heart is vast, you both can fit into it, but I know that no man will accept such a situation, and rightfully so. I know I'm wrong. Tell me, Aman, what should I do?"

Aman reiterated his point, "I understand your point, Chandni, but please don't worry about me. You reside in my shadow, and you're never far from me."

Chandni found some peace. Just then, the doorbell rang. Chandni bid goodbye to Aman and went to the door. As it opened, Chandni stood amazed. "Sagar.. What a pleasant surprise," she said, seeing Sagar standing with a large bouquet of yellow flowers.

"Couldn't resist.. I was restless all night. I love you, Chand..." Sagar completed his sentence, closing his eyes, and Chandni embraced him.

Today, Chandni felt a new poem in Sagar's touch. His lips were writing an epic on Chandni's lips. Sagar and Chandni remained lost in each other for hours.

In the evening, as Sagar left, Chandni talked to Aman again. This cycle continued for a few days. Sometimes Chandni began to worry about herself. The flood of emotions was slowly nullifying Chandni's heart and mind. Chandni was being ground in the mill of her own created emotions while talking to Aman late into the night, sometimes, in between, Sagar's call would come, and Chandni was being crushed in the mill of her own feelings.

Chandni wants both Aman and Sagar. Their friendship had become the joy of her life. But why couldn't she break free from the societal mindset that loving two people at the same time is wrong? Even if society didn't care, her own mind wasn't giving her permission. On one hand was Sagar's innocence, his belief in standing by Chandni like a rock in every situation; on the other hand was Aman's voice and personality. There was no shortage of love anywhere. Even if the thorn of the balance of the scales pierced her soul, the weight of their love didn't weaken.

Chandni never wants to get married. She always wants to live life as an independent woman. Her ambition in the field of literature has always been there. She always feels that after getting married, the four walls of the house leave no time for anything else. The expectations of in-laws, the duties of a wife towards her husband, and the responsibilities of children, this becomes a woman's life after marriage. Even after that, whether the husband is happy or not, there is no guarantee. Chandni cannot forget the tragedy of Rajni's life.

But today, the same Chandni wants to dedicate herself to one life. She wants to wear the traditional red vermillion on her forehead. It was the thought of freedom and modernity that got Chandni trapped in such an emotional maze today. She felt that for an emotional mind, dedication is needed, not freedom; love's bond, not independence; modernity is good only when it's under control.

Aman or Sagar, the dilemma! Chandni wants to spend some time alone. She wants to dialogue, dialogue, and dialogue with herself. She wants to spend some time away from both Aman and Sagar. Both of them accepted her desire.

Four days passed in complete silence. Chandni stayed at home. Anu was busy due to her exams. On the fifth day, Sagar's voice started echoing on the phone in the morning, and Chandni said, "Sagar.. Hi... Missed you so much.. I told you that I need a week of solitude, absolutely alone."

"Yeah, babe.. I know," Sagar said innocently, "But am I not human, why didn't you stay away from me? Punishment is yours for the test, why me? Chand.. I'm coming.. please."

Chandni started laughing after hearing Sagar's words and said, "Oh.. come on.. but quickly. I miss you too."

Within ten minutes, Sagar was standing at Chandni's door. "Sagar.. What a pleasant surprise," Chandni exclaimed.

Sagar placed his lips on Chandni's lips, took out a ring from his pocket, and put it on Chandni's finger.

"What's this?" Chandni asked in surprise.

"Today is our anniversary, Chand... Last year, on this day, I had my first meeting with you at the Nehru Centre, and you came into my life like a breath of fresh air," Sagar said poetically.

"What a gesture, Sagar.. Your way of expressing love is unique too.. When did you come to Southampton?" Chandni asked Sagar, expressing her joy.

Looking down, Sagar said, "To tell you the truth.. I've been in a hotel in the street in front of your house for two days. I see you coming and going to Anu's school every morning and afternoon. If not a conversation, at least your sight, didn't that break your prohibition?"

"Love you, Sagar, really love you," Chandni embraced Sagar.

Two weeks passed, but there was no call from Aman. Chandni was a little worried, she called Mumbai, "Hey Aman, where are you? Why are you so quite!"

In response, Aman said, "Well.. you didn't call, so I kept quiet too. You needed time, didn't you? By the way, I was just about to call you these days."

"And how was your busy time, everything okay?" Chandni asked.

Aman said, "Well.. very busy, got some new contracts. Most of the time was spent in recording."

The conversation didn't last long. Chandni felt a bit distant in Aman's conversation. But there was no deep impact of this on Chandni's heart, she went out for a walk in the garden. The weather was changing. The appearance of buds and the greenery on the trees were giving the message that summers are coming. Summers mean the arrival of guests in England, the organisation of musical programs. Chandni's promotion company has booked eight events this year in the summers. Shows are going to be held in all major cities like London, Birmingham, Manchester. The arrival of artists from India, America, and Europe will be there. Chandni was lost in these thoughts when Sagar's message came, he was going to America for ten days. Chandni felt helpless for a moment. Maybe she also wants to go with Sagar. Sagar spent the whole evening with Chandni before going to America. Chandni feels happier with Sagar than before. He takes care of Chandni more than before, and takes care of Anu.

Anu started to see Sagar as her friend. When they sat together, Sagar acted completely like Anu's age, and both behaved like children.

Sagar's flight might not have even reached America yet, and Chandni had already called twice to the hotel where Sagar was staying. Chandni herself was surprised at her own disturbed state in Sagar's absence. She had never felt such an attraction towards Sagar before.

On the other hand, Chandni's conversations with Aman had decreased. Chandni felt that Aman wasn't making any special effort to come closer to her. Either he was trying to distance himself from Chandni's life or he couldn't accept Chandni and Sagar's relationship practically, and somewhere his ego was bothering him.

Meanwhile, Sagar returned from America within seven days instead of ten. After reaching Southampton directly from Heathrow Airport, he once again captivated Chandni's heart. Now, Sagar didn't talk much about Aman either.

Chandni teased, "Sagar.. I feel so lonely, I miss someone a lot."

With a sarcastic smile, Sagar asked, "Oh.. really? who?"

Lost in Sagar's question, Chandni said, "You.. only you.."

Scorned

Simran doesn't want a brother; she wants a sister. "Boys are so naughty. Besides fighting, jumping around, and yelling, what else do they know? Everyone in the house wants a boy. Grandma is obsessed with boys, as if girls have no value. She herself is a girl. Mom is good. She also wants a girl. She adores me! She keeps saying that girls are very sweet, like Simran." "Auntie is also crazy. She doesn't know what joy she'll get from her nephew. When he pulls her hair and throws balls at her, then she'll realise how mischievous boys can be. Oh God, give me a sister, a dear sister. I will love her so much. Just like Mom ties my hair and dresses me up, I'll also dress her up like a doll." Nurturing her innocent thoughts, Simran, a seven-year-old girl, talks to herself and falls asleep between her mom and dad.

In the morning, Simran is awakened not by her mom but by her auntie with great enthusiasm. "Wake up, Simran, wake up quickly, we have to go to the hospital. Your brother is coming." Simran gets up with a giggle and starts getting ready quickly to go to the hospital.

On reaching the hospital, Simran finds out that her sister has arrived, and she couldn't contain her happiness. She gazes at her newborn sister with extreme affection despite everyone's disappointment, trying lightly to touch her and eagerly wanting to hold her in her arms. That's when Simran's ears catch her grandma's words. "Look at the difference between the two sisters. Simran's complexion and this girl's! It's like night and day. No one in our family is this dark. Where is Simran, fair and lovely, and where is this black duckling born from?" Aunt was also echoing similar sentiments. "This girl doesn't seem like Simran's sister at all. If a girl had to be born, she should have been born like Simran. In front of this black one, Simran looks like a Hollywood heroine." Simran is puzzled. On one hand, she feels good hearing praises about herself, but on the other hand, she doesn't like the way they talk about her sister. Without understanding the difference between dark and fair, Simran internally rejoices, saying to herself, "Mom didn't have a boy, that's why they talk bad about my sister. God has listened to me, I have a sister; I have won, and these people have lost."

Not only auntie and grandma, but visitors also engage in such comments, escalating

Simran's dilemma. The best part for her is her mom's statement, "I love both my daughters equally. If Simran is a Hollywood heroine, then my little daughter Rakhi is no less than a Bollywood queen. Look at her features... she's no less than Rekha." With time, Simran and Rakhi's age kept increasing. Simran began to realise the importance of her fair complexion not only among family members but also amongst schoolmates and friends. "Hey, Dinesh, Simran will have to have a *swayamvar*. Not only India but half of England will come to ask for your elder daughter's hand. But for Rakhi... start saving some money for her. Without a dowry, nobody will accept her hand," says Asha.

"Asha, what happened to your little daughter? Was there a shortage of coconuts and oranges in India? Seems like you were very careless during the second pregnancy," retorts another. Phrases and comments like "One sister is Anglo-Indian and the other is Negro, one an angel and the other a servant, one princess and the other a maid," made both sisters grow up with their own thoughts and emotions.

Simran's sense of superiority and superiority complex grew, and Rakhi struggled with feelings of inferiority. On Simran's 16th birthday, a big party was organised. Many of Simran's friends came home for the first time.

Rakhi is now nine years old. She felt as if Simran didn't want to introduce her to her friends. This was true, Simran felt embarrassed about her sister's dark complexion. Rakhi began to feel Simran's disdain even from small things, often mocking her.

Rakhi had to face occasional discrimination at school due to her complexion, but she was the favourite of most of her teachers. Her sweet nature and dance performances won everyone's hearts. She enjoyed participating in plays and dramas on stage.

At the age of twelve, Rakhi got the lead role in the annual function of her school. She played the character of an Asian girl who becomes a victim of racial discrimination in a school in London, in the stage adaptation of the story 'The Undeclared Miss World' written by Dr. Satyendra Srivastava. Rakhi received much praise from people, but Simran made fun of her, saying that because of her dusky complexion, she suited the role of an Asian girl.

Speaking innocently, Rakhi said, "Sister, the teacher was saying that she is trying to arrange for this play to be staged in London. I will also go with them." To this, Simran replied, "You and London, they don't let anyone enter there. No one will let you in." With time, Simran's pride regarding her fair complexion grew, and due to people's comments and her own arrogance, she began to feel that she wouldn't find a suitable match in India, and she would marry a boy from England or America. Simran's behaviour was disrespectful even with other family members.

Through the internet, Simran's desire was fulfilled, and she found an English boy who came to India on Simran's insistence, and he agreed to marry her. Simran didn't listen to her family and married Robert, the Englishman, in court and went to London.

Simran achieved what she wanted in life. Because of her fair complexion, she received more love from her grandma and auntie than other family members, praise from friends, and now, the desired groom.

Robert is the manager of a good bank in London. He has a flat in the posh Chelsea area and is well respected in society.

"I am so lucky, Rob, to have found a handsome man like you," Sim said. "And I am so lucky, Sim, to have found a romantic wife like you," replied Robert.

Complimenting each other, Robert and Simran start their new life together. Robert tells Simran that his parents have organised a party at their home in Manchester to celebrate their wedding, and they need to leave for there in two days. Simran is also very excited to meet them. Robert buys a new dress of her favourite brown colour for Simran for the special party.

Robert's father organises the party in the large lawn of their house. Robert and his mom start introducing Simran to the guests. Simran initially feels good, but soon she starts feeling lonely as everyone gets busy with their own groups.

Seeing Simran alone, Robert comes to her and holds her hand, taking her amidst the people. He says to Simran, "Feeling bored? Mix with people, slowly you'll get to know everyone."

"I know, don't worry," Simran replied with a smile.

To initiate a conversation with some people, Robert asks, "Friends, how do you like Simran's dress? I got it for her." Upon hearing this, Robert's mom adds from behind, "And who else could it be, we all know how much you love the brown colour... that's why you brought a brown wife from India."

Robert manages to laugh it off, but Simran doesn't like the tone of Robert's mom's comment.

A little later during dinner, Robert asks his mom's friend, "How is Sherry? Didn't she come today?" The woman replies, "Don't talk to me about her, she's involved with a black guy whom I don't like at all."

"So what, my wife is also Indian, my mom didn't have any problem," Robert retorts. Making a face, the woman says, "Your mom might be Mother Teresa, but I'm not." Simran doesn't feel good about these conversations. She starts feeling uncomfortable with these people.

A few days later, Simran hears similar things at a party of one of Robert's friends in London.

"Hey mate, your '*Paki*' wife is so sexy." "Rob will have brown kids now." "Rob has got some red wine in his cellar, offer him some white dear."

Returning home, Simran expresses her discomfort to Robert about such comments. Robert says, "Forget it, Sim, just chill... it's all just jokes."

Simran feels really hurt by Robert's attitude. She complains in a sarcastic tone, "Is my humiliation a joke for you?" "Relax Sim, neither can I change your colour nor shut people's mouths," Robert replied curtly.

Gradually, Simran begins to realise that she will have to face such taunts if she wants to live in London. Once considered a princess in India, Simran has now become a *Paki* after marrying Robert. She becomes hesitant to attend parties with Robert. Simran's pride and confidence starts to crumble. The same fair complexion that Simran was so proud of in India becomes a reason for her humiliation in London every day. As days go by, Simran spends four years in London. After coming to London, Simran misses her family, but she has not maintained any special contact with them in India.

In India, everyone thinks Simran is a proud girl who doesn't want to keep in touch with them, and they are unhappy with her because she married against their wishes. Simran starts feeling very lonely. Robert wants Simran to go out with him and mingle with people, but she insists on staying away. Robert spends late nights at parties, and Simran stays alone at home. Simran hates the racist remarks, but it doesn't affect Robert. With these issues, the distance between Simran and Robert grow.

One day, Robert says to Simran, "Sim, I know you don't like my parties, but today is special. It's my promotion party, and I would feel good if you come too." Simran had been waiting for such a proposal from Robert for many days. She agrees but says, "Yes, I will, but if anyone makes a racist remark or discriminates, I will leave the party." Laughing, Robert says, "Okay, I will make sure nothing like that happens."

The party is held in a luxurious hotel in London. During the party, Robert's boss, Mike, takes Robert's hand and congratulates him on his promotion, saying, "Today, Robert is our special guest. All of you please take care of him and his wife. Please refrain from making any racial comments."

Simran feels as if she's on fire. She finds herself in an awkward situation. She wants to go and slap that Englishman hard, but she has to bow down and thank him instead.

After the party, she tells Robert, "Rob, you and your English society can't think of anything beyond colour, colour, and colour... this obsession with skin colour is so important to them." Laughing sarcastically, Robert says, "I think, Sim, you are highly complexed and paranoid. You unnecessarily become irritated by such things and are filled with negativity. If you have so many issues with English society, why don't you go back to your country? What's the problem with being a brown person in a British race? Who called you to this society in the first place? You always wanted to marry an Englishman."

Simran is shattered by Robert's response today. For the first time, she saw this side of Robert. Throughout the night, Simran kept crying and regretting running after her fair complexion all her life.

Robert kept sleeping late into the morning. Simran came out of the bedroom and sat down with a newspaper. Suddenly, her eyes fell on the picture on the third page. Simran was shocked.

The picture was of her younger sister Rakhi.

Under the picture, it was written, "This year, Rakhi from India has won the title of Miss World."

Your Shivani

Shivani's world had changed. From the daughter of a middle-class family, Alok Nath's daughter, to a high school teacher, Shivani is now the daughter in law of millionaire Seth Mohan Lal Mehra and the wife of business tycoon Akash Mehra. Outside her room, Shivani sits on a swing, lost in thoughts, smiling to herself. Today her dream is coming true as her poetry collection, 'Your Shivani ', is being launched.

As Shivani converses with herself, she thinks, "I never imagined my collection would be published. How happy everyone in Raebareli will be. *Babuji* (Pt. Deen Dayal) will be most pleased, whose presence and inspiration led me to write poetry. The eminent scholars of Hindi are stepping out of their shells for the first time, only at my request. I remember, they used to lead every discussion in the school campus. Their critique breathed life in my poetry. Many students taught by *Babuji* are now in high positions, but he remains the same. Look at me, I've only been to Lucknow twice with Father, I've only seen Mumbai in movies, but today Mumbai-Kolkata is no less than London-Paris."

Suddenly, there's a knock on the door, and Shivani rushes to open it.

As the door opens, the anticipation reflected in Shivani's eyes begins to dissipate, and a wave of emotions floods in. "*Babuji*," she says, touching Pt. Deen Dayal's feet and bringing him inside.

"Stay blessed, dear," Pt. Deen Dayal says, looking at Shivani 's grand room, "Even after reaching such heights, you remembered me. Keep progressing."

"No, *Babuji*, I owe you more than Father. Without you, I couldn't even have thought about the launch of my book," Shivani says.

The effect of Shivani's words is evident in Pt. Deen Dayal's smile.

"How was your journey, *Babuji*?" Shivani asks.

"The journey was uneventful, just spent some time searching for your servant at the station," Pt. Deen Dayal replies.

Shivani starts feeling guilty; Akash or she could have gone herself to pick up Pt. Deen Dayal. Shivani remains silent and leads Pt. Deen Dayal to his room.

"*Babuji,* please wash your hands and face, I'll arrange breakfast," Shivani says as she heads towards the kitchen.

By noon, Akash also arrives home.

"Hey, Shivani, Pt. Deen Dayal is here? Hope all is fine," Akash asks.

Shivani, taken aback, says, "Oh, you're here so early!"

"Why not? Today is the launch of my Shivani's book. Can't I share these happy moments with my wife?" Akash replies.

Shivani is overwhelmed with joy, "I thought after marriage, my poetry would end, but you, you turned out to be such a fan who never even read my poetry, yet you ensured my book was published."

"What are you saying, Shivani," Akash says, holding Shivani 's hand, "I live because of you. The day your father brought the proposal for our marriage and said they have Saraswati (Goddess of knowledge), not Lakshmi (Goddess of wealth), I felt as if my fate was sealed. My father accepted his daughter-in-law without even seeing her."

"Forget about all this," Shivani says, "Tell me, what's the plan for today? Who all are coming for the launch of my book?"

"Don't ask, you know, the Mayor of Mumbai will grace your book's launch. Not just Mumbai, but many prominent journalists and writers have been invited," Akash replies.

Shivani can't seem to contain her happiness. The clock strikes the appointed time; Akash, Shivani, and Pt. Deen Dayal head to the five-star hotel in Mumbai. The launch ceremony is about to begin.

As Pt. Deen Dayal looks at Shivani in awe upon seeing the grandeur of the hotel, Shivani remains silent. As they enter the magnificent premises of the hotel, cries of "Hey Shivani, Hello Shivani, let's meet Mrs. Mehra" echo through the hall. Shivani gets lost in the crowd. Pt. Deen Dayal sits quietly on a chair by the side.

For the first time, Shivani has stepped out of Raebareli for a literary event, getting acquainted with Mumbai's poets and writers.

"Shivani, meet Mrs. Suman Ambani, the managing director of Suman Floor Mills and Suman Textiles, a renowned Hindi storyteller. Her book 'Childhood in Japan' has received two national awards."

"Interesting," Shivani said with great humility, "were you going to Japan to write this book or..."

Interrupting Shivani, Suman Ambani said, "No... no... I was returning from California to India. My plane was delayed for three hours in Tokyo, and I saw some Japanese children at the airport. I couldn't resist and started writing this book."

Shivani was deeply astonished—a person understanding Japanese culture in just three hours! It reminded her of the time when a songwriter from Raebareli, Abhimanyu Adhir, was asked to write songs for children in a TV documentary. He spent two weeks sitting in a park near the children's school, trying to understand their emotions... And... *Babuji...* Pandit Deen Dayal Ji, who wrote epics and epic of poetry about the independence movement, never received any awards. His poetic compositions, which inspired millions of youths to fight for freedom, remain unappreciated to this day. Such sacrifice... such dedication...

Suddenly, Shivani overhears a conversation between two women, "Mrs. Patel, your husband has created such a buzz. The buildings of your construction company are making Mumbai so modern and beautiful. And yes... your necklace is exquisite, it looks antique."

"Correctly observed, Ragini. I got it from Christie's auction in London," replied Mrs. Patel.

"Oh, when did you go to London?"

"Last year, I was invited by a British publisher to write about the lives of the poor neighbourhoods and residents of Mumbai."

Shivani drifts into deep thought again. What would those who demolish homes of the poor to erect towering buildings write about their lives?

" Shivani, this is Mr Rajendra Ambar, the editor of your book and the organiser of today's event," a man introduces Shivani.

"Namaskar, Shivani Ji, your writings are truly profound," Rajendra Ambar speaks to Shivani.

"Thank you very much, I am grateful to you for considering me worthy," Shivani says.

"It's all thanks to Mr Mehra. Our newspaper runs on his advertisements," says Ambar, triggering some thoughts in Shivani's mind. Then she sees Pandit Deen Dayal in the corner and says, "Come, Ambar Ji, let me introduce you to *Babuji*. It is his inspiration and blessings that taught me how to write poetry. The epic poems of Hindi scholar Pandit Deen Dayal Ji remain relevant even today."

Though Ambar meets Pandit Ji, he quickly moves on without giving him much importance. Shivani doesn't like this and realises that in the world of those who get awards through money and contacts, the literature of people like Pandit Deen Dayal remains unappreciated and in darkness. She sits next to Pandit Ji and says, "Had some soup, *Babuji*?"

Pandit Ji replies, "Yes, my child, take care of yourself."

Shivani remembers the gatherings of Raebareli when seven people would share four cups of tea and some snacks she often brought from home. Maybe Pandit Ji was thinking the same.

Then an announcement in English comes on the mic, "Dear friends, I would like to invite the Chief Guest, the Mayor of Mumbai, and Mrs Shivani Mehra."

With Pandit Deen Dayal Ji's blessing in mind, Shivani confidently walks towards the stage. In her mind, she wonders, "What is this? Launching my Hindi poetry collection in English? No... no... this cannot happen. What will *Babuji* say? I should tell Ambar now." But there was no opportunity to meet Ambar anymore. Amidst the applause, Shivani heads straight for the stage.

As the program begins, Shivani's anxiety eases a bit when she hears Ambar speaking in Hindi. There was no mention of Pandit Deen Dayal Ji's contribution in his welcome speech. There was no discussion about the importance of literature in life. Shivani remembers when Pandit Deen Dayal Ji rejected the proposal to become the vice chancellor of Delhi University and decided to stay in Raebareli, simply because he wouldn't have time to devote to literature in Delhi, even though he would get money and honour there. He often said that without selling flower garlands in the morning, a gardener's son cannot go to school. Many talented children from poor backgrounds remain deprived of literacy.

The Mayor of Mumbai gives her speech, but there is no mention of Shivani's collection in her discourse. She only talks about the business achievements of Ambar and some wealthy investors and journalists present there. The mayor's speech pierces Shivani's heart like a needle.

Then Rajendra Ambar invites Mrs Suman Ambani.

Mrs Suman Ambani begins her address by reciting some Sanskrit verses. Shivani's gaze falls upon the wrinkled forehead of Pandit Deen Dayal Ji, and she understands that there is an error in Mrs. Suman Ji's pronunciation.

Mrs Suman Ambani says, "I am pleased that today compositions are being written even in palaces. In the poems of Shivani, there is the pain of a labourer working in the scorching heat of May-June and the agony of an old man sleeping on the footpath in the biting cold."

"No this is not true, Shivani's mind screams out, My compositions are mostly written in

Raebareli, they belong to a simple girl from there, not to any wealthy person. Why are people giving more importance to wealth than literature here?

But Shivani finds herself utterly powerless.

The time comes for Shivani to be invited on stage to speak about her process of her writing.

In such an atmosphere, what will Shivani be able to say, what will she be able to read? She doesn't know. Still, hiding the feelings of incapability on her face, she approaches the microphone and begins her address, "There are no compositions of a wealthy person in 'Your Shivani,' they are the emotions of a girl from a small town of Raebareli, the experiences of a life she hasn't just seen but felt. The description of scorching heat in my poems, the mention of chilling cold is because I've grown up in its lap."

Without any external facade, Shivani starts revealing the truth of her heart, "I am grateful to the publishers who have turned my poems into books. I never intended to write poetry deliberately. Whenever the pen starts moving on its own in my hand, a poem is born. I have used imagination in my poems to reveal the truth, I haven't written poetry for entertainment or fun, my poetry is the expression of my emotions, my pain. In my compositions lies the knowledge given by my *Babuji*, Pandit Deen Dayal Ji, my devotion to him, my worship."

Shivani, standing alone amidst the crowd, addresses Pandit Ji directly, "My book 'Your Shivani' is dedicated to Pandit Deen Dayal Ji, who is present here today." As she says this, she steps down from the stage towards Pandit Ji. All the listeners in the hall stand up, leaving their seats aside, their eyes moist. For a moment, Shivani's gaze meets Pandit Ji's, and she reads a new line of love in his eyes.

Shivani, placing her book 'Your Shivani' at the feet of Pandit Deen Dayal Ji, says, "*Babuji*, please accept my worship."

Pandit Deen Dayal's misty eyes are overflowing with emotions, ushering in a sea of blessings, birthing a new poetry of souls.

Acceptance

Six years have passed, Ankit has begun to understand the reflection of society. It's the year 1971 and Ankit knows India and Pakistan are enemy countries. He understands that Congress and Jan Sangh are opposed to each other, his mother is very good but not dear to his grandmother, his uncle uses foul language too! Its okay for grandfather to smoke *Beedis*, but uncle is forbidden to smoke cigarettes, watching movies is considered bad but listening to stories is good! If the father throws the plate in anger, ignore it; but if the glass breaks from your hand, a slap on the cheek is certain.

At the age of learning, punishment was becoming a habit, and learning not to become like adults!

It was better to have my stuttering tongue, nobody took it seriously. If they understood the emotions of my childlike heart, maybe they would have felt embarrassed! That veil of less knowledge was better, today, at the age of fifty five, I want to speak the truth of childhood, but maybe innocent words are inappropriate now or perhaps I lack that innocent courage!

Hafiz was my best friend. When he used to come home with me, grandmother and aunt wouldn't like it but mother had no objection. This mystery took years to understand and unravelled when I turned eleven. Hindu-Muslim conflicts started in the city. Schools closed and meeting Hafiz became impossible. Everything calmed down in a few weeks and schools reopened but meeting Hafiz didn't happen. He stopped coming to school. A few days later, I found out that he had been admitted to another school. It was the holiday of Eid that day. But evening came and *sevaiyan* (sweets) didn't arrive from his home. I questioned grandma who scolded me just like my aunt did and mother just appeased me by saying, "If you like *sevaiyan*, I'll make it next week." Why next week? It's Eid today, but I had no answers.

After dinner, I sat down at the dining table and asked again, "Isn't there *sevaiyan* for dessert today?" Everyone remained silent but Papa said eagerly, "You want *sevaiyan*? Come," he took it out from the bag, handed me a box and said, "Here, take the *sevaiyan*, it's from Javed uncle's place!" I happily enjoyed the *sevaiyan*.

Still, all night I searched for the answer to this question: Why weren't *sevaiyan* made at my house on Eid when *Gujiyas* on Holi, sweets on Diwali were not only made but distributed. Then why not on Eid?

I couldn't resist any longer and asked Papa in the morning, and then I understood that I am Hindu and Hafiz is Muslim. Eid is a festival of Muslims and Holi-Diwali of Hindus. At the age of eleven, I understood the difference between Hindu and Muslim.

My friend Hafiz is a Muslim and I am Hindu. So why did his mother send gifts to me on Diwali? Why were the *laddoos* sold outside Hindu temples that were his favourite and why did he tie *rakhi* to Manisha in school? I had so many questions but none of the elders had the answers and I understood that time alone will answer my questions; not Mummy, Daddy, aunt or grandmother!

Time began to weave my answers at its pace, untangling the tangled yarns like a sweater.

At the age of thirteen, I had a bicycle to go to school. Riding here and there on the bicycle, passing through new streets, searching for new paths, the joy of my childhood began to rise. One day, suddenly I heard a voice from behind, 'Ankit, Ankit,'I applied the brake on my cycle and looked back to see Hafiz standing.

Seeing Hafiz almost two and a half years later, I began to feel strangely amazed and a wave of happiness ran within me. Hafiz started jumping seeing me. We met with great affection. The series of meeting Hafiz and I started again but only once or twice a week. Hafiz no longer lives in that neighbourhood where he used to live before. Two years ago, his house was burnt down in Hindu-Muslim riots. He had to go to his aunt's house in another area with his family. It is a Muslim-populated area of the city, so Hafiz's father wanted to live in a safe area. They were so scared of the riot that his father took Hafiz away from school and got him admitted to a *Madarsa*.

Knowing all this made me restless. Hafiz and I belong to different religions, that's what Papa told me but why are we so different that our education is in different languages and so are the books? If we come face to face in a riot, can we kill each other for our religions? My own friend is so different from me, then why does he love me so much, and why do I like him so much?

I began to feel trapped in my own questions. Then in my eighth standard, the result of junior high school came. I passed with very good marks. Papa was very happy and proud of me. He took Mom and me to dinner at a big restaurant.

Papa eagerly asked me what I wanted as a gift. Perhaps Mom must have told him that these days my eyes are on a Moped. But something else was going on in my mind. Watching my silence, Mom said, 'Ankit, say what's in your heart, Papa is in a mood today. Take advantage of it!'

What I asked for, its sadness ate me up inside for many days. I had asked Papa for answers to my innocent questions as a gift. The whole atmosphere had sunk into seriousness. I made him unknowingly saddened. I still remember, forty-three years ago, the sentence Papa said to me that evening. 'Son, I don't have the ability to fulfil your demand today. I don't know any shop from where it can be bought,' I couldn't understand why my questions were so difficult for the head of the science department of the city's biggest university? From childhood, if I asked Mom for anything, I got the same answer, tell Papa and he'll bring it. How did my powerful Papa weaken today because of my questions?

My questions hadn't yet settled deeply when one day, my father came to me and began, "Ankit, come, I want to show you something."

"Want to show something?" There was no enthusiasm in my father's voice, just a deep-seated plea echoing in his troubled expression. He placed a letter in front of me and said, "Read." Upon my inquiry, he explained that the letter had come from Iqbal Bhai in Pakistan.

As I began to read the letter, "Brother Rakesh, how are you? How are things in India? Here, things are much better now, and we hear that a new government has formed in India. Our two nations' ministers will meet soon. There will be a significant agreement, and obtaining visas for us will become easier. It's been thirty years, my friend, and I miss you all a lot. Last week, on my birthday, as always, Ammi applied a *tilak* on my forehead in your name. My little daughter, upon seeing the *tilak*, bombarded me with questions. She's turned four and has started speaking her mind. 'Why don't I get a *tilak* on my birthday? Don't girls get *tilaks*? Abdul Bhai doesn't get a *tilak* on his birthday either. Do only fathers get *tilaks*?' With great difficulty, Ammi explained to her and narrated our story."

Along with the letter, my father began to tell me Iqbal Bhai's story. Iqbal's family was our neighbour before the India-Pakistan partition. Iqbal and my father were born on the same day. There was a great friendship between both families. Iqbal and my father went to the same school, had lunch together, and celebrated birthdays together. Often, they even wore similar clothes. During the riots and partition of 1948, Iqbal's grandfather decided to go to Pakistan. And we were separated. Your grandmother believes that during the riots, your grandfather was killed because of Iqbal's uncle.

I had never seen such sadness in my father's voice before. For a moment, I was afraid of his choked throat. Today, my father's words answered many of my questions. However, there was no full stop at the end of those answers, only a semicolon, birthing new questions. I decided never to burden my father with my questions again.

Tomorrow is my daughter Neha's wedding to a Muslim doctor, and he's Pakistani too! I am happy for her but many of my friends and relatives are unhappy! The new generation - carefree! The question remains - until when will these grievances persist?

Journey

Gender and complexion were my first identities. A boy was born, fair-skinned at that!

From the moment of birth, my identity began to form.

"A boy? Congratulations!"

Everything was so new, new people, a new language, a new environment, yet it felt as if I was born with an understanding of the world in a middle-class family in a small town of India.

On the first day of my birth, "You're so lucky, a fair-skinned boy is born, not as dark as your elder brother Kailash!" "Just look at his fingers, they're long, he'll become an artist!" "Oh, look at the sparkle in his eyes, this boy, he's a charmer!" "The hair on his head seems a little less, looks like it's hereditary!" "He laughs at everything, he'll become a joker!" The priest said, "He is born under the auspicious stars of *Navratri*, he'll rule!" "Move aside, move aside... he's my son, I'll make him a doctor!"

I didn't have the skill to say "Mother" with my tongue, nor was I familiar with the "A" of the alphabet just a few hours after birth and yet I understood enough to know that they were talking about me which reflected in their eyes. There was a lot of calculated hope in their minds. With birth, it was decided as if my future, my reality, my identity, my work, my name, my values were destined by them. By the time I was five to seven years old, school became the mirror of my life!

Fair complexion, tall for my age, lanky body with curly hair and brown eyes: I was the favourite boy of the family , teachers and neighbourhood. This was perhaps a reflection of judging the book by its cover and unaware of my internal weaknesses and struggles.

They didn't know that I struggled with reading and writing. I understood everything but it took time. I had dyslexia. A condition I didn't know, nor did anyone else... I was just a source of amusement for some and ridicule for others!

I didn't even know that I belonged to a lower caste. By the time I was seven or eight, I began to understand the reality of poverty and discrimination. Not only that, the fourth and fifth standard in school made me realise that I was only attractive to look at but weak from within!

At sports day in my school, teachers would put me on duty at the tea and *samosa* stall, and everywhere there would be talks and praises of those children who many times in school canteen or social parties were ignored by the girls in my presence. Those same short, dark, chubby boys would surpass me today because I was flat-footed. Running was difficult for me.

I began learning to hide my weaknesses in my pocket and the art of moving forward.

Now I have two younger sisters as well; my father started getting sick and my elder brother has a habit of intoxication so amidst responsibilities, I started moving towards high school exams.

It's okay, I'll make every effort to fulfil my duties.

Duties - Sisters' marriage, brother's care and progress of family which in simple terms would mean that I should get married; father a few children and responsible for passing on the values taught by my elders to the next generation.

Before I could understand the meaning of my existence, I was the principal of life's experiences.

Any question, any confusion, I had all the answers. I have eighty years of experience now, am a successful man, family man, good businessman and culturally rich from every perspective!

The whole city respects me, but I haven't risen yet from my weaknesses - dyslexia, lower caste, loser with flat feet nor the stigma of being from a poor family!

I'm not an ordinary person, I was born a warrior. Today, my daughter is a doctor in America, both sons are engineers in Germany. No one asks them about their caste.

Times have changed, my family is happy and prosperous.

Yes, happy and prosperous, in my eyes! I'm nearing eighty, and tomorrow is my last day of this life. This day was decided, I just found out today!

"Is there anyone who can tell my children that I'm leaving, come to meet me."

Everyone wants to come, but time is very ruthless. Just like on the birth of my daughter, I was drunk under the intoxication of alcohol, slept in the pub, and my wife went to the hospital alone in the autorickshaw; just like on the birthdays of my sons, I used to just give them money for gifts and indulged myself in business activities or sometimes in frivolity!

Lord Krishna said in the *Gita*, the soul is immortal, the body is a garment! The soul changes bodies and there is a new birth, in a new body. Lost in such thoughts, I don't know exactly when my eyelids closed. A deep, very deep, long sleep prevailed.

One morning, I heard a faint sound in my ears; a language that I couldn't decipher at all. When I opened my eyes there were all new faces around! New people, new environment; a new birth had happened to me.

What name to live by now, what expectations to fulfil, new duties, new responsibilities, new traditions, a new God, a new culture and new religion! A new journey has begun again! Am I on the journey, or is the journey within me? Where am I, really? The name given is all that I am. I am not the soul; I am the body, and this body is my identity; such an identity that keeps changing with my being. Identity which changes with the body. I and my identity are none, the identity is just of the body; in which the soul resides like an occupant, or the body resides in the soul like a tenant!